# Nest

## by Bathsheba Doran

# SAMUEL FRENCH

FOUNDED 1830

NEW YORK HOLLYWOOD LONDON TORONTO

SAMUELFRENCH.COM

ISBN 978-0-573-66356-7          Printed in U.S.A.          #16127

## IMPORTANT BILLING AND CREDIT REQUIREMENTS

NEST by Bathsheba Doran
Signature Theatre (Arlington, VA) April 24th – June 24th 2007
Directed by Joe Calarco
World Premiere

*NEST* was commissioned Signature Theatre, who requested a play inspired by the true story and Ballad of Susanna Cox. *NEST* had its World Premiere at Signature Theatre in Arlington, VA on April 24, 2007 under the direction of Joe Calarco with following cast and crew:

Cast (in alphabetical order):

JOE . . . . . . . . . . . . . . . . . . . . . . . . . . . . . . . . . . . . . . . . . . . . . Michael Grew
ELIZABETH . . . . . . . . . . . . . . . . . . . . . . . . . . . . . . . . . . . . . . Vanessa Lock
CHAPLAIN . . . . . . . . . . . . . . . . . . . . . . . . . . . . . Stephen Patrick Martin
JACOB . . . . . . . . . . . . . . . . . . . . . . . . . . . . . . . . . . . . . . . . Charlie Matthes
DANIEL BOONE . . . . . . . . . . . . . . . . . . . . . . . . . . . . Richard Pelzman
DRUMBLE . . . . . . . . . . . . . . . . . . . . . . . . . . . . . . . . . . . . James Siaughter
SUSANNA COX . . . . . . . . . . . . . . . . . . . . . . . . . . . . . . . . . . . . . Anne Veal

Understudies:

DRUMBLE/CHAPLAIN . . . . . . . . . . . . . . . . . . . . . . . . . . . Paul Danaceau
JACOB/DANIEL BOONE . . . . . . . . . . . . . . . . . . . . . Christopher Janson
SUSANNA/EI IZABETH . . . . . . . . . . . . . . . . . . . . . . . . . . Melora Kordos
JOE . . . . . . . . . . . . . . . . . . . . . . . . . . . . . . . . . . . . . . . . . . . Joseph Thanner

Scenic Design . . . . . . . . . . . . . . . . . . . . . . . . . . . . . . . . . . . James Kronzer
Costume Design . . . . . . . . . . . . . . . . . . . . . . . . . . . . . Kate Turner-Walker
Lighting Design . . . . . . . . . . . . . . . . . . . . . . . . . . . . . . . . . . . . . . Chris Lee
Sound Design . . . . . . . . . . . . . . . . . . . . . . . . . . . . . . Matthew M. Nielson
Production Stage Manager . . . . . . . . . . . . . . . . . . . Katherine C. Mielke
Production Manager . . . . . . . . . . . . . . . . . . . . . . . . . . . . . . . Chris Akins
Dramaturg . . . . . . . . . . . . . . . . . . . . . . . . . . . . . . . . . . . . . . . Irina Brown
Assistant Director . . . . . . . . . . . . . . . . . . . . . . . . . . . . . . . . . . Sara Sahin
Directed by . . . . . . . . . . . . . . . . . . . . . . . . . . . . . . . . . . . . . . Joe Calarco

## CHARACTERS

**JACOB GEER** – mid-30s
**ELIZABETH GEER** – his wife, mid-30s
**SUSANNA COX** – their indentured servant, early 20s

**A CHAPLAIN** – 40s
**DANIEL BOONE** – a pioneer, in his prime

**MR. DRUMBLE** – a publisher, late 50s - early 60s
**JOE** – a writer, early 20s

## PLACE
In and around Philadelphia

## TIME
1808-1809

## NOTES

The play is to be performed without an intermission. In Part 2, the three movements require a fluid expression of time and space. The intent is impressionistic not realistic.

The text of the *Ballad of Susanna Cox* is the original text that was sold at her hanging. Daniel Boone's song "The Cuckoo's Nest" is an old British folk song which later evolved into an Americanized cowboy song. The version in the play includes a final verse sung by Daniel and Susanna which I wrote myself.

" 'Twas in truth an hour
Of universal ferment; mildest men
Were agitated; and commotions, strife
Of passion and opinion fill'd the walls
Of peaceful houses with unquiet sounds.
The soil of common life was at that time
Too hot to tread upon; oft said I then
And not then only, 'what a mockery this
Of history; the past and that to come!'"

William Wordsworth, The Prelude, 1805

"Another thing, Willie, while we are on this subject. *(Pause)* The sadness after song. *(Pause)* Have you run across that Willie? *(Pause)* In the course of your experience? *(Pause)* No? *(Pause)* Sadness after sexual intercourse, one is familiar with of course."

Samuel Beckett, Happy Days

*For my friend, Polly Lee*

# PART 1

## Scene 1

*(A dark kitchen in the middle of the day.* **SUSANNA COX,** *her work set aside, masturbating, quietly, efficiently. An animal mindlessly seeking release, crouched.*

**JACOB** *enters, holding a jug. He watches for a moment.)*

**JACOB.** Susanna?

*(She stops immediately)*

What are you doing?

*(a beat)*

**SUSANNA.** Nothing.

*(a beat)*

**JACOB.** I need more water upstairs. I spilled what was left in here.

*(She takes the jug and fills it, her back to him. He watches. Eventually, she hands it back. Jacob doesn't move.)*

**JACOB.** Is that something you do often? In the kitchen?

*(a beat)*

**SUSANNA.** I think you mistook yourself.

*(a beat)*

**JACOB.** *(a whisper)* I won't tell anyone.

*(A beat. He exits.)*

## Scene 2

*(Jacob's study, high up in the house. Books and papers
crowding his desk.*

**ELIZABETH** *scans the bookshelves, looks through papers
on his desk.*

**JACOB** *enters with the jug.)*

**JACOB.** I thought you went out.

**ELIZABETH.** The meeting was cancelled. I'm just looking
for your copy of "The Adventures of Daniel Boone."

*(**JACOB** gets it from the shelf and hands it to her.)*

**JACOB.** It's bad.

*(**JACOB** looks through some papers, apparently ready to
get back to work.)*

**ELIZABETH.** Jacob… I actually only came in here to borrow
this, but…

I saw a letter on your desk. I read a few words before I
even knew what I was doing.

*(She takes the letter from his desk)*

"I find I wake, reluctant to rise, confident the day will
be filled only with loneliness…

I carry out my daily activities as normal, and nobody
has noticed that my spirit has left me. I don't know if
it will return."

*(Pause.)*

**JACOB.** I was actually only writing to Lewis, to ask if he
knows of any work. I don't think I'll send it.

*(a beat)*

**ELIZABETH.** No, I certainly wouldn't send it if you're asking
for work.

*(a beat)*

**ELIZABETH.** Is there something I can do?

**JACOB.** Nothing.

*(a beat)*

**ELIZABETH.** You are isolating yourself. You've stopped coming to church. You ignore the farm. You have stopped taking your morning walks...

**JACOB.** In Philadelphia I was working with a number of prominent politicians –

**ELIZABETH.** No you weren't...

**JACOB.** I was!

**ELIZABETH.** You were not, Jacob! It isn't work if you aren't being paid! As I remember it, mostly what you did was sit in the City Tavern with them and drink.

**JACOB.** That's where everything happened!

**ELIZABETH.** When we met you were quite happy, I seem to remember, at the thought of living in the country and running the farm. Quite happy, I remember, at the thought of living in nature, now that the city, you said, had got so crowded and dangerous, was so prone to disease. Quite excited you said, for the time to think and read and write, which is what, you insisted, you did best. And I seem to recall that you were running out of money, unclear how to earn any, and were quite thrilled when you saw the size of this house!

*(She gets her breath back.* **JACOB** *opens his mouth to speak but she cuts him off.)*

**ELIZABETH.** *(cont.)* It's not my fault Jefferson offered you no place in government, and it's not my fault that your thoughts are not always enough to keep you entertained all day. As you had previously believed.

*(a beat)*

You could take more of an active role in running the farm. I wish you would.

**JACOB.** I stopped taking an interest years ago. I noticed it made no difference, they do very well without me. I am trying to help our farm by writing a pamphlet addressing America's agricultural future. I shall send it to Mr Drumble in Philadelphia. Although I doubt he'll publish it. He ignored the last three things I sent him. I have become invisible.

**ELIZABETH.** Because you are isolating yourself! We're only fifty miles from Philadelphia! Go to town more!

**JACOB.** And do what?

Jefferson hasn't written in almost three years. No more has Lewis or Madison.

*(a beat)*

Europe's producing the greatest philosophers since ancient Greece at the moment and where do they all meet up? A stone's throw from the house my father was born in. Sometimes I wish my parents had stayed in Switzerland.

*(Pause.)*

**ELIZABETH.** I would take you to my meetings, Jacob, but they are only for women.

**JACOB.** Why aren't there any meetings for just men?

*(a beat)*

Oh my mistake, of course there are. They're called politics.

## Scene 3

(**DRUMBLE** *alone on stage. He is giving a lecture at the University of Pennsylvania.*)

**DRUMBLE.** As of now, the English language contains only English poets. Shakespeare's gone. He is theirs. Marlowe is gone. Chaucer and John Donne and Milton are gone. Theirs. And who do we have?

We have the great authors of our constitution, a document I published myself. We have Mr. John Filson he author of "The Adventures of Daniel Boone" which has sold most satisfactorily. But what we haven't got is a Plato!

Who will be our Homer? Who our Euripides, who our Socrates and Sophocles? I think we can live without another Aeschylus...

I read a new play this morning, currently being performed in Paris. There is an American character in it. He is the villain. Murdered by a group of wealthy widows that he has failed to seduce in the final act.

(*a beat*)

The scene is supposed to be comic. We can no longer depend on Europe for art. Europe no longer understands us

We are currently without a voice and I consider it a national emergency. America must be written. She longs to be articulated, she craves form and meaning. In the last three years, our country has doubled in size. Here in Philadelphia we have all watched as our population has tripled in size as the Athenians watched, when Athens sprung up around them. Someone must describe this new place. My guess is that someone in this room has already begun. Because in a gathering of twenty or more there is always at least one secret poet. One who explores the secret properties of letters. An alphebetist. An alchemist. There is a poet in this room, I know there is. Or perhaps you write prose. Sitting by your window, night after night, weaving magical tales with your fingertips. Whoever you are, send whatever you're writing to me, as quick as you can. I will read plays, poems, stories, novels, even the beginnings of novels. Because although you may think yourself a future doctor, or lawyer, or farmer of these United States, you may also be the first great American poet and not know yet that you are the man we will one day hold up to the world, and say look who sits with Shakespeare! Look who sits with Homer and the Greeks! He is of *American* soil! This is his book! And in it he offers you our souls...

## Scene 4

*(Outside. Night.* **JOE** *waits.* **DRUMBLE** *enters.)*

**JOE.** Mr. Drumble? Great speech. Very inspiring.

*(a beat, gesturing his manuscript)*

These are some poems.

**DRUMBLE.** You are a student at this university?

**JOE.** Yes, sir.

**DRUMBLE.** What are your poems about?

**JOE.** Birds, sir.

*(a beat)*

**DRUMBLE.** How interesting. The theme of wilderness is what drew me to the story of Daniel Boone.

*(a beat)*

The concept was mine. I commissioned the author to create a narrative of Boone's legendary adventures. There are so many stories still to tell about the wilderness. Different stories. One about a boy like you... or what about a father, trying to make a home for his family, alone in a cabin, surrounded by wolves. Or is it a pair of brothers, twins, trying to start up a farm and making friends with savages?

Listen...

*(They listen.)*

**DRUMBLE.** The new world is waiting to be described.

*(a beat)*

There will be a first great American poet. For all we know... what's your name?

**JOE.** Joe.

**DRUMBLE.** For all we know, Joe... it's you.

*(a beat)*

Such moments dreams are made of. My dreams. In which I meet the first great American poet and he hands me his manuscript on a moonless night.

*(A beat.*

**JOE** *hands him the manuscript.)*

**DRUMBLE.** Then I leave to catch a carriage.

*(And* **DRUMBLE** *exits.)*

### Scene 5

*(Jacob's study. Day.)*

**JACOB.** I think you know why I've called you in here.

*(a beat)*

It's about what I saw in the kitchen.

*(a beat)*

Remember?

**SUSANNA.** I had an irritation...

**JACOB.** You were rubbing at yourself.

**SUSANNA.** Yes, sir.

**JACOB.** On the kitchen floor.

**SUSANNA.** Yes, sir.

**JACOB.** Because of an irritation?

**SUSANNA.** It is an ache.

*(a beat)*

What will you do to me?

**(JACOB** *takes a moment before launching into his pre-prepared speech.)*

**JACOB.** The solitary act is a common response to a feeling of pressure in the lower regions. The feeling is not uncommon. However, performing it will not relieve your symptoms, as you may have noticed. It will only make them worse.

I have three excellent medical text books on the desk, and when it comes to the solitary act they all say the same thing. Don't do it. It is unhealthy and danger-ous. It may cause vision and hearing difficulties later in life. If it becomes a compulsion it can lead to insanity, apparently. So it has to stop. It is not just a matter of the kitchen, Susanna. I am talking in general. It is at your age precisely... how old are you?

*(a beat)*

Haven't you kept count? I don't blame you... well

you were eleven when you came here so....you must be... what twenty four? Really? I always think of you as younger...

*(a beat)*

I must get back to work as well. Very busy. Writing a new pamphlet. About agriculture in the new states. Now that Jefferson's doubled the size of this country we have to work twice as hard.

**SUSANNA.** *(leaving)* Yes, sir.

**JACOB.** Would you like to see a map?

*(He shows her a map)*

This is preliminary, not all of these details are confirmed. The cartographers are waiting on the sketches of Lewis and Clark. They were supposed to have been made public over a year ago.

*(a beat)*

I met Jefferson, you know. Before he was President. And Lewis was a friend. Have you heard of him? The one who went up the river? With Clark?

*(a beat)*

At one point I thought I might go out there with him. But the expedition received limited funds so... no.

**SUSANNA.** Have you heard of Daniel Boone?

**JACOB.** Daniel Boone? The frontiersman? Of course.

**SUSANNA.** Do you know him?

**JACOB.** No, why would I?

**SUSANNA.** *(shy)* I heard...

**JACOB.** What did you hear?

**SUSANNA.** When there was Cook... when I was little... she told me... he was born just a mile away... just a mile down the road his house stands.

**JACOB.** You're right. That's true. He was born in a cabin less than a mile from here. Elizabeth met his father, I think. When she was a little girl. I have a book here, somewhere, about his adventures. You're welcome to borrow... oh Elizabeth took it... Do you read, Susanna?

**SUSANNA.** No.

**JACOB.** Oh.

*(a beat)*

There's Kentucky on the map. See?

**SUSANNA.** Where Daniel Boone lives now?

**JACOB.** Exactly. All this is ours now... We have to start thinking about how we're going to govern out there.

**SUSANNA.** The Indians?

**JACOB.** The Indians? No, the Indians are perfectly happy as they are and we can leave them be. We have to think about the Americans that are going to move there. We have to set up some rules.

**SUSANNA.** Can't they make their own rules?

**JACOB.** No, that's a bad idea.

**SUSANNA.** Why is it?

**JACOB.** Never mind. It's a very controversial issue.

*(**SUSANNA** stares at the map.)*

**JACOB.** What did you feel? When you were touching yourself.

**SUSANNA.** I said.

**JACOB.** An ache?

*(a beat)*

Then what?

*(a beat)*

Had I not walked in, what would have happened?

*(a beat)*

When you touch yourself, what happens?

**SUSANNA.** I can turn my body into water.

*(a beat)*

**JACOB.** When I was a little boy, my father caught me, as I caught you. I was in an area in my boyhood house where we kept the coats. Why one cannot do such a thing in the privacy of one's own bedroom, I know not, but I remember that after I discovered the practice I also felt a compelling urge to do it in every room in the house. He mocked the size of my… apparatus. And then told me, that if I continued to pull on it, it could come off. And then I stopped. Mostly. Not entirely.

    You've got me wondering now if Elizabeth has done it. Perhaps we are all doing it together alone. All over this house. What a sad and hilarious image.

    *(a beat.)*

**SUSANNA.** The sin you saw, I commit it daily. Three times daily, sometimes.

**JACOB.** Susanna?

    May I kiss you?

    I don't want to hurt you. I don't want to get you into trouble. Or me into trouble. I just… I'd like to kiss you. May I? Can I kiss you?

**SUSANNA.** Yes.

    *(They kiss and stay kissing longer than either one of them expects.)*

## Scene 6

(**JOE** *sits in Drumble's office, waiting for the verdict on his poetry.*)

**JOE.** I just want to know if I'm any good.

(**DRUMBLE** *looks at the poems.*)

**DRUMBLE.** Sonnets? Sonnets, Joe?

**JOE.** Yes.

**DRUMBLE.** Leave the sonnets to the English. You'll never better them anyway. What are you going to do? Write a better sonnet than Shakespeare?

**JOE.** No, sir.

**DRUMBLE.** Your tone is very pleasing. Optimistic. But measured. Tone cannot be taught.

*(a beat)*

When do you graduate?

**JOE.** This year.

**DRUMBLE.** Will you continue to write? Do you have an independent income?

**JOE.** I am to work for my father.

**DRUMBLE.** Doing?

**JOE.** It is related to the manufacture of nails.

**DRUMBLE.** I see.

*(a beat)*

Well, keep writing, don't give up. You're young. At your age it is perfectly natural to imitate. But I can do nothing with sonnets. As far as I'm concerned you should never write a sonnet again.

**JOE.** I've been working on something else. I have been exploring a character.

**DRUMBLE.** What kind of character?

**JOE.** A young man, like you said, who goes out into the wilderness.

**DRUMBLE.** Does he have adventures?

**JOE.** He has a fight. With a coyote.

**DRUMBLE.** Send it along, Joe. Send it along.

*(a beat)*

And if I like your character then you and I may go on a journey together. Like Lewis and Clark. Up the river, in search of the source of the ocean. And we will survive it as they did, like brothers, even when the labours before us seem Herculean in prospect. Because we both want the same thing.

## Scene 7

*(Late afternoon.* **JACOB** *and* **SUSANNA** *undressing each other.)*

**JACOB.** You look like a ghost in this light...Of course you only look like a ghost if ghosts are white. We have no idea. I had a friend who swore he had invented a contraption that allowed him to see spirits and he said they exist in many hues, he described them as a sort of floating palette and said the differences in color reflect differences in temperament. He may have changed his thesis by now. We lost touch.

All the work being done in that area is very, very interesting.

Did you know work was being done in that area?

**SUSANNA.** No...

**JACOB.** I am a skeptic, I think. But I rule nothing out.

*(***JACOB*** goes down on* **SUSANNA***.*

**DANIEL BOONE** *enters.)*

**DANIEL.** That feels good, does it?

Got to admit, I'm a little jealous. Feel that old demon jealousy rising up in me...

*(a beat)*

But I know you're awful lonely. I get lonesome sometimes. Under all those stars.

**SUSANNA.** Yes...

**DANIEL.** I'm just passing through. I'm headed back to Kentucky, right now. Wish you could come with me.

**SUSANNA.** Yes...

**DANIEL.** I guess now's not a good time.

**SUSANNA.** Stay there...

**DANIEL.** We're all waiting for you.

My whole family's waiting for you round a big oak table.

I've got ten strapping sons, Susanna.

Any one of them would take you in a heartbeat.

And you know I want you.

Can't wait to hold you. Pin you down. Touch you.

SUSANNA. Soon...

DANIEL. You're gonna be with Old Daniel Boone real soon.

We're gonna go on walks together, under the stars, then we're gonna cook.

You catch a rabbit and you've got yourself a feast.

I'm gonna teach you how to hunt for your own self, gonna teach you how to build a cabin in the woods. Gonna learn you Indian wisdom about why the trees grow and what the birds are singing about. Might meet the Shawnee King one day. And we'll kill him too, if he comes running at us. Steal his horses, ride out into the wind, hair flying back.

And you're gonna be alright.

Wish you'd hurry up and get there.

Are you bringing him?

SUSANNA. I don't think so.

Might need someone though. Don't have a gun.

DANIEL. Don't he have a gun?

SUSANNA. No.

DANIEL. Asshole.

SUSANNA. He can come with me.

DANIEL. Whatever you say, sweetheart.

SUSANNA. Yes.

DANIEL. He'll protect you on the journey.

SUSANNA. Yes.

DANIEL. And when you get there it will be the three of us then.

I tell you what, there's enough horses for everyone out there.

The three of us could ride on one horse together. I seen it happen.

You're nearly there, sweetheart, you're nearly there, you're nearly there. You're gonna get to me, we're gonna be there together, you're there, you're there, you're there.

*(SUSANNA orgasms.)*

**DANIEL.** The Adventures of Susanna Cox.

**SUSANNA.** Daniel?

When are you going to teach me what the birds are singing about?

**DANIEL.** Just as soon as you start walking. All you've got to do is follow the setting sun.

*(DANIEL exits. They recover.)*

**JACOB.** My wife never lets me see her like this.

**SUSANNA.** Like what?

**JACOB.** Plain.

*(Pause.)*

**SUSANNA.** I've got a question.

**JACOB.** And what is it?

**SUSANNA.** Am I a slave?

**JACOB.** No, of course not. We paid your father for you. That doesn't happen with slaves.

## Scene 8

(**ELIZABETH** *outside. Flowers in her hair, Pan-like. She has "The Adventures of Daniel Boone" under her arm. The* **CHAPLAIN** *sees her.*)

**CHAPLAIN.** Elizabeth?

**ELIZABETH.** Your violets are out along the path.

**CHAPLAIN.** Just standing in the rain?

**ELIZABETH.** Oh, it's hardly raining. It won't last.

**CHAPLAIN.** Yes, it's still bright out. It's sprinkling. Good for my violets.

**ELIZABETH.** Good for everything.

**CHAPLAIN.** Your book's getting wet.

**ELIZABETH.** I don't care if it does. I thought it was very badly written.

**CHAPLAIN.** What is it?

**ELIZABETH.** "The Adventures of Daniel Boone."

**CHAPLAIN.** Hated it. I have no idea why it's so popular.

**ELIZABETH.** I know! What is so heroic about rummaging around in the wilderness like a hog?

**CHAPLAIN.** I have no idea.

**ELIZABETH.** Marian kept saying it was local history. I said in real life the man is seventy years old and wanted for debt. That wasn't mentioned anywhere. Now she's got our whole group reading it. I wanted us to read Gibbon.

**CHAPLAIN.** You wanted your ladies to read "The Decline and Fall of the Roman Empire?"

**ELIZABETH.** They're not particularly my ladies, and yes, why not? People read Gibbon. I have read some myself. But apparently for some, studying civilization isn't as interesting as the ramblings of a wild man up a tree.

(*a beat, leaving*)

Good luck with your violets.

**CHAPLAIN.** Give my best to your husband. It's been so long since I've seen him.

**ELIZABETH.** I know.

*(a beat)*

He's suffering at the moment. With questions. He'll be alright again. It's hard for him out here, sometimes.

**CHAPLAIN.** Would you like me to talk to him?

**ELIZABETH.** No. Not yet.

**CHAPLAIN.** He has time. You're both young and healthy.

**ELIZABETH.** People think we're young because we have no children, but we're not.

*(a beat)*

We are growing old together.

## Scene 9

*(Drumble's office.* **DRUMBLE** *is reading aloud Joe's story to* **JOE.***)*

**DRUMBLE.** "Adam lay down next to the fire and looked up at the stars. The bite from the Coyote ached, but the flesh was already healing thanks to the poultice he'd made, and having roasted and eaten the animal, he no longer bore it any grudge."

Good for him.

"He wondered how many more days it would take him to reach the settlement on the Ohio river, and as he calculated the miles still remaining, he fell asleep. He awoke seven hours later to a pale sun, and three Indians, sitting on the ground quite close to him, chewing on the coyote's bones."

*(a beat)*

I find that a very powerful image.

*(a beat)*

"He didn't move and they didn't notice him so Adam lay still for a moment, thinking how best to deal with the situation. What did they want? Was it only food? Or some ominous other purpose? But if they meant him harm, why wasn't he dead already?"

Good point.

*(He continues reading)*

"How long should he wait to find out? He watched them feeding."

And this is neither here nor there, but your handwriting is most pleasing to the eye. You have no idea how exhausted my eyes can get trying to make out the illegible scrawls of some of the men who work here. I fully expect to retire blind.

"And suddenly, according to no particular sign, they scattered, each running in a different direction. When Adam sat up, they were gone."

*(a beat)*

Very good. This is very, very good.

**JOE.** Thank you.

**DRUMBLE.** Nothing has happened, yet I want to keep reading.

*(a beat)*

Did you have an idea of what might happen next?

**JOE.** Well, eventually… after some time… first, I thought next he would continue walking… and see things… it is a meditation on solitude. At this point.

**DRUMBLE.** I can imagine a series of stories about young Adam. Every week a new adventure. The story would begin with the conclusion to last week's adventure, and then lead us right into the middle of another. So with this one, we would end the moment Adam awakes surrounded by savages. He puts his hand on his gun.

*(a beat)*

Only next week would we learn that he wasn't harmed. What do you think?

**JOE.** Clever.

**DRUMBLE.** I love the name Adam. First man. That's clever.

**JOE.** Thank you.

**DRUMBLE.** I will pay you for a story about young Adam each week. That would cover a roof over your head here in town, and a little more besides. If you grew tired of young Adam someone else could take over. You would write me something else. That's how it works here. If you're interested, then I want you to go out the door, turn left, walk along the corridor to the third door on the right. Open it, you'll see a room, and in it a little man called Alan. There he will furnish you with all sorts of things that may be useful to you as you embark upon your new life as an independent young man about town, including money.

**JOE.** Yes, sir. Thank you, sir!

*(a beat)*

One piece of advice. Don't become a rogue. Many of
my writers take on a roguish quality which I don't like.
There's nothing clever about it.

## Scene 10

*(Elizabeth's dressing room. Bright morning.)*

**ELIZABETH.** I find the current obsession with topography since Lewis and Clark quite baffling. Suddenly everyone is fascinated by the shape of leaves.

**JACOB.** Because we've got a lot of trees we didn't know about. We've got a significant number of new species we didn't even know existed.

**ELIZABETH.** Like what?

**JACOB.** We've got an animal called a buffalo. You eat it. They're like cows. In fact, they also make cheese. We can send away for some, there's an order form in one of my pamphlets.

**ELIZABETH.** It won't taste good.

**JACOB.** How do you know?

**ELIZABETH.** It's just something I know. Susanna can you come here for a minute?

*(SUSANNA enters.)*

**ELIZABETH.** I want to ask you both something.

*(a beat)*

How would you feel if we were to house a runaway slave?

*(a beat)*

**JACOB.** I think it's a good idea.

**ELIZABETH.** Really?

**JACOB.** Yes.

**ELIZABETH.** At my group today, we are supposed to discuss the idea in principle. The practicalities of where they would live, what we would feed them, how dangerous it would be. And were advised to consult with our household. Test the waters.

**JACOB.** I'd be all for it.

**ELIZABETH.** Where would we keep him. In the house?

**SUSANNA.** In the barn?

*(a beat)*

**ELIZABETH.** That's all Susanna. Thank you.

*(**SUSANNA** exits.)*

**ELIZABETH.** We can't keep a man in the barn. Can we?

**JACOB.** It might be a whole family.

**ELIZABETH.** No, that's too much. How long would they stay, anyway? Never mind. I shall find out the details today. We are to be addressed by a Quaker.

**JACOB.** Did you know she can't read?

**ELIZABETH.** Who, Susanna?

**JACOB.** I offered to lend her a book, she told me she can't read a word.

**ELIZABETH.** Well of course she can't.

**JACOB.** I thought she might have learned. Before she got here.

**ELIZABETH.** From who? I met her father, I doubt he could read either. At least not in English. He was German.

**JACOB.** Really?

**ELIZABETH.** Didn't you meet him?

**JACOB.** No.

**ELIZABETH.** He was a German Mennonite. Long beard.

**JACOB.** She's a Mennonite?

**ELIZABETH.** Yes. Technically. Why this sudden interest?

**JACOB.** Because there's me and all my books, and you and all your social projects, and it suddenly occurred it me that we have an illiterate woman in our own house. That's not right.

*(a beat)*

I wonder if we ought to teach her.

**ELIZABETH.** To read?

**JACOB.** Her tenure's up soon. I thought it would be nice if we released her into the world a little more advantaged than when she arrived here.

*(a beat)*

Or do you plan to keep her on?

**ELIZABETH.** I don't know. I hadn't thought about it yet. I'd rather keep her than find somebody new, I suppose.

**JACOB.** I think we should give her the choice.

**ELIZABETH.** This isn't like you. Keeping up with the household details.

**JACOB.** We certainly wouldn't want to keep her here against her will. You sit on an abolition committee for goodness sakes.

*(a beat)*

**ELIZABETH.** No of course not. I suppose I'd better talk to her.
Frankly she's better off here. Unless she wants to marry. And while she was waiting for someone to ask her, I honestly don't know if her father can afford to feed her.

**JACOB.** I don't know, maybe it's silly, I just suddenly started thinking that you and I could perform a rather radical experiment. Educate her, dress her a little better. You could take her out and introduce her to some of your ladies. After all, this isn't Europe. There ought to be some flexibility.
It's up to you of course. You would be mostly responsible.

**ELIZABETH.** And in the meantime would she continue to work for us? Would I take her to a lunch, and then bring her home to cook supper? It's a very odd idea.

**JACOB.** I thought it might be a little project for us to do together.

*(a beat)*

We have no children. I thought this might be nice.

**ELIZABETH.** You seem so much happier.

**JACOB.** I am.

**ELIZABETH.** Why?

*(a beat)*

**JACOB.** I don't know. The weather maybe? I even thought I might go for a walk today.

*(**ELIZABETH** kisses him suddenly and hard.)*

**ELIZABETH.** When winter comes this year let's use each other for conversation more. I think that was the problem last year. Somehow we just fell silent, didn't we?

*(**JACOB** nods. )*

Of *course* the dark months are the hardest. Of *course* they are.

*(She exits.)*

## Scene 11

(JACOB *and* SUSANNA *frantically trying to achieve sexual satisfaction without having sex. She pushes him away. Unsatisfied.*)

JACOB. I have to work, anyway.

SUSANNA. So do I.

JACOB. I *want* be inside you. I wish I could be...

(*a beat*)

What about something else? What about from behind again? Did you like that?

SUSANNA. It's not proper.

JACOB. Not proper? But did you like it?

SUSANNA. No.

(*She cleans.*)

JACOB. Your tenure's almost up, you know.

SUSANNA. You want me to leave.

JACOB. (*exasperated*) I'm just thinking of you.

(*a beat*)

What do you want?

SUSANNA. I want to follow the stream outside the house. Keep walking. See where it goes. To the ocean maybe. Pass through Kentucky...

Do you know anyone who lives out there?

JACOB. Susanna, the people out there are practically living in trees!

SUSANNA. Want to live there.

JACOB. What would you do out there? How would you live? Where would you live?

SUSANNA. I'd need money.

JACOB. I don't have any money. The farm brings in enough for our clothes, our food, and books. That's it. We have very little to spare. It's a fact. Elizabeth keeps the books, but I've seen them.

SUSANNA. *(looking out)* She's coming back. Walking across
    the fields.

JACOB. Get away from the window then.

SUSANNA. I'm supposed to be in here. Supposed to dust.

    *(a beat)*

    Do you put it inside her?

    *(a beat)*

JACOB. Sometimes. She can't have a baby.

SUSANNA. Maybe you can't have a baby, ever think of that?

    *(a beat, she touches him)*

    I feel it prodding at me. Wants to come in.

JACOB. Go downstairs, now.

SUSANNA. There's time.

JACOB. That's enough! I have work to do as well. Jefferson
    could retire any day and this still isn't written! And if
    he doesn't ban slavery in the new states all he'll have
    left us with is a great big space and a great big question
    mark. It's irresponsible! And that's why I don't have
    any money to give you. We can't make a profit if every-
    one else uses slaves! It's impossible!

    *(A beat. He's frightened her.)*

SUSANNA. I'm supposed to dust...

JACOB. Leave it. I'll tell her I didn't want to be disturbed.

## Scene 12

(**DRUMBLE** *is reading at his desk, tired, eyesore.* **JOE** *stops by, with a manuscript. He sits, puts his feet on the desk, which* **DRUMBLE** *notes with displeasure.*)

**JOE.** I have my young Adam story.

**DRUMBLE.** *(taking the manuscript)* Ah, good. How is he?

**JOE.** Very well.

**DRUMBLE.** How close to the settlement?

**JOE.** *(evasive)* Quite close.

**DRUMBLE.** I really think it's time for him to leave the wilderness now. It's time to start exploring life on a settlement.

*(He starts hunting around)*

I have various first hand accounts. Diaries and letters, people send me. "Some observations." That's all people ever send me. Observations. As though I can publish everybody's observations all the time. I'm not *that* democratic.

*(He hands* **JOE** *a stack of documents)*

There are more filed somewhere.

*(a beat)*

In a year young Adam could be married. I'd like him to have children. He would still have adventures but they would be based in the settlement. The whole thing would be more complicated.

**JOE.** Alright. He'll be in the settlement next week.

**DRUMBLE.** Good.

**JOE.** What are you reading?

**DRUMBLE.** The first chapter of a novel. A woman sent it in.

**JOE.** Any good?

**DRUMBLE.** I think so. Listen.

"Charlotte rose at six that morning, and walked around her block. She did that every once in a while, if she awoke early, and sensed adventure. This particular morning, her walk proved to be one of the best of its kind. Something in the conflation of the sun and the hour resulted in a moving picture of the rarest beauty that she alone was witnessing and knew would soon be gone."

It's good, isn't it?

**JOE.** Not bad.

**DRUMBLE.** I can't do a thing with it, unless she sends more. I occasionally do receive first chapters from the ladies. But then nothing.

**JOE.** No discipline.

(**JOE** *gets up to leave.*)

**DRUMBLE.** Do you still write, Joe? Your own work?

**JOE.** You keep me very busy.

**DRUMBLE.** Don't give up, Joe. Don't get tired. At any moment, there could be an explosion within you. And you will create!

## Scene 13

*(Elizabeth's dressing room.)*

**ELIZABETH.** I've wanted to talk to you, Susanna.
You were contracted to us by your father twice. The second contract will reach an end in less than a year. You arrived a child. You are a woman now.

*(a beat)*

If you wish to stay it can be arranged. You're familiar with our routine and we all get along. However, my husband thinks you may want to broaden your horizons. He wants me to ask you what you want.

*(a beat)*

I would imagine you want a lot of things. Most of them won't be possible. We were born into the wrong bodies.

*(a beat)*

My husband has an idea that he would like to educate you which might allow you to find a better post, or perhaps a husband with a little money.

*(a beat)*

Would you like to marry?

*(Pause.)*

**SUSANNA.** I don't want to marry a stranger.

*(Pause.)*

**ELIZABETH.** I have kept you away from the farm deliberately. But you are older now. Some of the boys who work on it are quite nice. And most of them unmarried. We could arrange for some social meetings at first. You would need time to assess personalities. See who you liked. We would put you in prettier clothes. Do something with your hair…

*(She studies **SUSANNA**.)*

SUSANNA. Ma'am? Am I too old?

ELIZABETH. No, not necessarily. In any case there's no reason to tell people your real age if you don't want to.

*(a beat)*

I could have married anybody I wanted to really, because I came with a farm. My father was quite rich for a time. When we lived in Philadelphia. And there would be parties and I would go and all the young men were paraded before me. And I chose Jacob. Against all counsel. Because he was so passionate about everything. He made the world seem full of possibilities. He didn't have any money. But of course that didn't matter. Because I did. So we got married, and moved here. And from that day on, nothing at all worked out as I'd thought it would. So I wouldn't be able to guarantee anything, Susanna. I can offer you something different, but not necessarily something better. And possibly something worse.

*(a beat)*

But if it's what you want then you should try and lose some weight. Because we shall be up against enough as it is.

## Scene 14

*(The* **CHAPLAIN** *sitting with his feet in a stream, fishing.* **JACOB** *sees him but it's too late for him to make a hasty exit.)*

**CHAPLAIN.** Jacob! So nice to see you.

**JACOB.** Thought I'd try to catch the last of summer.

**CHAPLAIN.** I had the same idea myself. Beautiful, isn't it?

**JACOB.** Very.

*(Pause.)*

**CHAPLAIN.** I received a letter today from a friend of mine who was sent by the church to be a minister to a small settlement in one of the new states. Missouri. He tells me there's much local excitement because some believe that the land they've settled on borders the exact location of the biblical garden of Eden.

**JACOB.** Is it possible?

**CHAPLAIN.** It's possible, I suppose. Although more of a cause for alarm than excitement, I should say.

**JACOB.** Why?

**CHAPLAIN.** Because we were cast out of Eden.

**JACOB.** Indeed.

**CHAPLAIN.** Unfortunately it was never anything more than a temptation that proved too much for us.

*(Pause.)*

We miss you at church.

**JACOB.** I've been very busy.

**CHAPLAIN.** Ah.

**JACOB.** Writing a new pamphlet.

**CHAPLAIN.** Oh. I thought someone else might have got to you.

**JACOB.** *(sitting)* Got to me?

**CHAPLAIN.** Well there are so many churches these days. The River Brethren. The Brethren of Christ. The Church

of God. The Amish. The Quakers are very popular, all
of a sudden.

JACOB. No.

CHAPLAIN. Good.

JACOB. It's just that I've lost my faith in god.

CHAPLAIN. Oh.

JACOB. That's it?

CHAPLAIN. You are not the first Jacob to wrestle with the
angels. You won't be the last.

(a beat)

But I'm sure you'll change your mind eventually. One
goes back and forth on these things through the years.
I wrestle with the concept of the divine myself sometimes. It's perfectly natural.

(a beat)

I was in Philadelphia recently, and everywhere there's
waste. Vegetable waste, the mess left from the horses,
human waste, and there's hogs everywhere, you can't
walk ten feet without tripping over a hog or stepping in
something unfortunate. Everything there has become
uglified somehow, even the people. But out here, in
the fields, I am reassured. I find it impossible not to
feel God in the sunshine, divine purpose in the crops.

JACOB. I'm afraid I consider that an illusion.

CHAPLAIN. Personally, I don't think people ever stop believing in God. I think they stop believing in hell. Or have
you been reading the new philosophers?

JACOB. I have.

CHAPLAIN. I thought as much. Their logic is very convincing.

JACOB. Logic is convincing.

CHAPLAIN. Jacob, it is by prayer and prayer alone that you
will come to know God. Not by reading French radi-
cals. Those of us in the business recommend that you
come to church every week, and pray with us, in a

group, even if you don't believe. It is through that process, you will find Him. Because, and I have to tell you this as a member of my flock, we believe that *not* doing so can be quite costly. In terms of the hereafter.

*(a beat)*

You know, there is a minister in New York who is said to perform miracles. He held his hands above a woman whose flesh was covered in sores. He remained that way for over an hour, and her wounds began to dry up.

JACOB. I would imagine that there's a scientific explanation.

*(Pause.)*

CHAPLAIN. Sometimes I catch myself thinking that the whole of the bible took place on a great big cloud and was never anything more than make believe made by God to make us believe. But then I remember it all happened right here on earth. Jesus was a man. Just like us. He struggled as we do, and raged as we do. They all did. Abraham. His father Terrah, who came home one day to a house full of broken idols and a son who claimed to have met the one true God. They were all just men. Like us. Struggling to know God. Here on earth. Which is why on this very globe you may find Golgotha, or Eden, or the skeleton of Noah's ark. Because it all happened right here. And it is still happening.

*(a beat)*

What made you turn away from God? What happened? What was the day?

JACOB. There wasn't a day. There's simply no evidence –

CHAPLAIN. You're wrong. I can feel God. I can feel him pulling me towards him. Is the path stony? Yes. Are my feet bleeding, yes. Am I starving and naked, is it dark and cold? You bet. But I know that's God up ahead, shining like sunrise. And when I die I'll be met on the other side by someone who loves me. And everything will clarify.

## Scene 15

*(All the characters on, or entering, the stage.)*

**ELIZABETH.** Ladies, I have been asked to lead today's discussion about "The Adventures of Daniel Boone." Who would like to speak first? Marian?

**JACOB.** *(to Susanna)* What's wrong?

**DRUMBLE.** *(to Joe)* What time do you call this?

**JACOB.** Are you sick?

**JOE.** I'm sorry...

**DRUMBLE.** Is your hair *singed?*

**JOE.** Yes, I –

**DRUMBLE.** *(angry)* What did I say?

**JACOB.** Did I do something wrong?

**DRUMBLE.** I said don't become a rogue.

**JACOB.** Why can't I touch you?

**ELIZABETH.** Did everyone like it as much as Marian?

**DRUMBLE.** You don't get to come to work late, just because you stayed out late drinking.

**JOE.** I wasn't drinking.

**JACOB.** Susanna? What's wrong with you?

**SUSANNA.** Nothing.

**DRUMBLE.** Is everything alright, Joe?

**JOE.** I just don't know if it's possible!

**DRUMBLE.** If what's possible?

**JOE.** To write something new!

**JACOB.** Why won't you let me touch you?
I miss you.

**JOE.** I was writing last night.

**DRUMBLE.** Writing what?

**JACOB.** Don't you want to be water together again? God, I want you to spill me all over the floor...

*(a beat)*

**SUSANNA.** There's a baby.

*(a beat)*

**JOE.** When I was writing it I thought it might be new. Like you said. An original form.

**JACOB.** We only did it once…

**ELIZABETH.** Honestly? I think the book is highly overrated.

**SUSANNA.** Look in the books.

**DRUMBLE.** Let me see it.

**ELIZABETH.** For one thing, it's badly written.

**JACOB.** What?

**JOE.** I don't have it.

**SUSANNA.** Look. In. The. Books.

**JACOB.** Why?

**SUSANNA.** So we can get it out!

**JOE.** I burned it.

**ELIZABETH.** For another, what is so heroic about rummaging around in the woods like an animal?

*(a beat)*

John the Baptist?

**DRUMBLE.** You burned your work?

**JOE.** I thought it was new and then I realized… I realized the influence. The whole time I thought it was something and it was nothing!

**JACOB.** *(skimming the page)* They don't always know why miscarriage happens… unlikely after quickening…

**SUSANNA.** Quickening?

**ELIZABETH.** John the Baptist didn't spend his days trying to kill things. John the Baptist didn't end up hiding from the law and disappointing his family…

*(a beat)*

Yes, I know he ate locusts, Marian.

**JACOB.** Is it moving around?

*(She nods.)*

**JACOB.** *(cont.)* Oh God…

**DRUMBLE.** Do you remember any of it?

**ELIZABETH.** I didn't mean to raise my voice. I apologize.

**JACOB.** Just calm down.

**SUSANNA.** We have to get it out.

**JACOB.** Just wait!

**DRUMBLE.** Don't look so disheartened! A man who burns his work can only be a poet!

**JACOB.** Miscarriage can be induced by a fall, or violence to the belly...

**SUSANNA.** Hit me.

**JACOB.** No.

**DANIEL.** Asshole.

**DRUMBLE.** What of it do you remember?

**SUSANNA.** Hit me!

    (**JACOB** *punches her.*)

**JOE.** "American wives chase hens at sunset...
Husbands walk home through American fields...
Barn sparrows nest in American architecture...
And the inventor dreams of a thousand nails...
As a thousand seeds blow west."

**DRUMBLE.** Again.

**SUSANNA.** Again.

    *(He hits her)*

    Again.

**JOE.** "American wives chase hens at sunset...
Husbands walk home through American fields...
Barn sparrows nest in American architecture...
And the inventor dreams of a thousand nails...
As a thousand seeds blow west."

**DRUMBLE.** But Joe... it *is* original. I love the form....

**JOE.** No, sir... It is in the manner of Mr. William Blake! Of England!

**DRUMBLE.** No! No! No! This is totally different to Blake! Blake sees only evil! You have written about good! The good of America! That's what I loved about you in the first place!

**JOE.** But you said a new form!

**CHAPLAIN.** I have a few announcements to make. Mrs. Philidia Crocker is sick with what is thought to be some kind of cancer of the bowel. I am sure she would appreciate any mention in your prayers. I actually meant to tell you that before the service.

(*JOE buries his face in his hand, desperately frustrated. DRUMBLE rubs Joe's back. A strangely paternal tender gesture.*)

**DRUMBLE.** I know you are frustrated. I said no more sonnets. Blake is our contemporary. It is a modern form. A modern form you have made your own. Joe...

**JOE.** I wanted to invent. I wanted to be the first.

**DRUMBLE.** If you finish this poem, if you finish it fast... I promise you Joe, you will be first.

**JOE.** First at what?

**DANIEL.** Susanna, have you bled yet?

**DRUMBLE.** The first great American poet.

**CHAPLAIN.** An anthology of Sermons is to be published by a Mr. Drumble in Philadelphia entitled "America: Prophecies from the New Eden." I have entered his contest and I have attempted to sound a Warning Bell in contrast to the blithe optimism of the title. If anyone has thoughts or suggestions before I messenger him the final draft, I would be happy to hear them after the sermon.

**DRUMBLE.** Blake or no Blake, it is a wonderful poem full of hope, full of dreams. It's what I've been looking for.

(*a beat*)

You need more time to write. From this day forward you will receive first refusal on our most lucrative commissions. No more young Adam for you. You need more money. With more money comes leisure and with leisure more time to create. You must try to recreate this poem –

**JOE.** But I burned it...

**DRUMBLE.** Who cares! Perhaps it was preordained and written in the stars. Start again! Second draft!

**CHAPLAIN.** And if these men are right, these men of science, these preachers, and politicians, if these men are right, and by a series of strange accidents, we find ourselves back in the place we were born, then the question becomes who are we that live here?

**SUSANNA.** What's that?

**JACOB.** From Philadelphia. The doctor said it's an old Indian recipe. He say's this happens all the time.

(**SUSANNA** *drinks the tea.*)

**CHAPLAIN.** Nothing but the children of those original inhabitants, the children of greed and copulation, the children of those that forsook God! And were forever cursed! Eden was never anything more than a temptation that proved far too much for us.

(**SUSANNA** *vomits.*)

**JACOB.** Oh God...

**CHAPLAIN.** It is in our nature to destroy.

**JACOB.** We need Elizabeth...

**SUSANNA.** No!

**CHAPLAIN.** Give us a garden and we will show you a graveyard. Because we are in exile from paradise! Unsure of God's love! Carrying our sin like a memory...

**ELIZABETH.** Jacob, Susanna has been throwing up all day. What if she has the fever?

**DRUMBLE.** In the meantime I would like to publish this fragment of yours. Against an illustration.

**JOE.** Of what?

**DRUMBLE.** Kentucky! A pastoral scene in Kentucky! Some of the boys recently put together a new pamphlet about the state of Kentucky to encourage good men, rich men, men of morals and authority to move there.

In sixteen blank pages they painted the most beautiful picture of the West that anyone ever saw. They have conjured Arcadia, Utopia, Kentucky! Your fragment of verse will be the final brush stroke. And from it we will take the title. I shall call the pamphlet "A Thousand Seeds Blow West!"

*(a beat)*

You will of course be compensated. And I shall tell the world to await the next installment! The next installment of your Epic of America!

**DANIEL.** *(to* **SUSANNA***)* See my shoes? Made from Indian skin. You've got to fight to survive, everyone knows that. The lion. The Indian. The soldier. Eagles kill their young. Rabbits too, if they're hungry enough.

**DRUMBLE.** Let's celebrate.

**DANIEL.** Peace is for the contented.

**DRUMBLE.** I will take you to the place where I used to drink with Franklin and try to convince him that the national seal had to be an eagle. "How can it be a turkey?" I'd bellow. "Turkeys can't even fly!"

**DANIEL.** You have to lie. Tell him you've bled.

*(a beat)*

There are things he's never going to understand. He's not the same as us and he won't help you. Remember how soft his hands are? The skin on his back, not a hair on it. Not a single hair.

**SUSANNA.** *(to* **JACOB***)* I have bled.

**JACOB.** Oh thank god. Thank god.

*(He moves towards her)*

I knew you would.

*(She moves away, shutting him out completely.)*

**SUSANNA.** We can't do this any more.

**JACOB.** I know.

## Scene 16

*(The scene changes.* **SUSANNA** *is outdoors. The moon is very bright. She looks around her. It's a whole new world. Everything she ever dreamed of.*

**DANIEL** *enters.)*

**DANIEL.** Isn't this nice? Both of us outside. In nature. Now, this is going to hurt.

*(***SUSANNA*** opens her legs. She begins to push the baby out.* **DANIEL** *is her midwife. She screams.)*

# PART 2

*(The Ballad of Susanna Cox begins as a cage descends on* **SUSANNA**. **DANIEL BOONE** *ignores everybody. He sits himself down and begins to skin a rabbit.)*

**EVERYBODY.** *(except Susanna and Daniel)*
Take notice now
Ye people all.
And hear what will be said
About a very gloomy case
Of a deluded maid.

She served as maid
In Oley long
With one named Jacob Gehr.
Her name was Miss Susanna Cox
I heard it mentioned there.

No education
She received
She knew but what she saw
The will of God she did not know.
Nor aught about his law.

The second month
And fourteenth day
Of eighteen hundred and nine
A child was born at half past four
Ere yet the sun did shine.

### FIRST MOVEMENT: THE PUNISHED

**CHAPLAIN.** *(to his congregation)* Who was Mary Magdalen? A prostitute. What does that *mean?* The most depraved act we can imagine... she may have performed. Imagine, please... Imagine now... imagine Mary before Jesus. What do you see?

*(a beat)*

You see Susanna Cox. You see a woman who didn't know how to live her life in His name! According to His word!

*(a beat)*

Susanna has but two weeks before she reaches the cliff at the end of the world. She will step out of her body. Lifeless, it will crumple to the ground.

*(a beat)*

Who will claim her soul?

*(**DRUMBLE** gives **JOE** a stack of papers.)*

**DRUMBLE.** Five ballads from the last five lady hangings in the East. Henny Finch, Jenny Hall, Mary Keen, Charlotte Jones....

**JOE.** *(reading, amused)*

"She took the knife! She thrust it in!

Twas cherry wine that made her sin!

She woke up drenched in blood and gore!

Her lover dead upon the floor..."

**CHAPLAIN.** We have to forgive her. Or none of us can get into heaven.

**DRUMBLE.** Which one's that?

**JOE.** That was Mary Keen.

*(Looking through the papers)*

What did Henny Finch do?

**SUSANNA.** *(mournful)* I murdered my babe by the light of the moon...

**DRUMBLE.** She also murdered her baby.

*(a beat)*

**SUSANNA.** *(a nursery rhyme)*
"Remember what your mother said,
Don't take the servant girl to bed
A servant needs but to be mastered
She doesn't need to bear a bastard."

*(a beat)*

**DRUMBLE.** First stanza, set the scene. Poor servant girl, uneducated. She's seduced, she becomes pregnant. We can't do much on the seduction. Just leave it up to the imagination. Then… the child killing. His innocent face, murder in the moonlight… the discovery of the body. Her confession. The trial. Her dreadful punishment.

**JOE.** It was a boy?

**DRUMBLE.** A boy.

**JACOB.** It was a boy.

**ELIZABETH.** I know. I know it was.

**DRUMBLE.** Twenty thousand copies, thirty-two stanzas. Quick as you can.

**JOE.** I'm surprised at you. Publishing a ballad.

**DRUMBLE.** Why?

**JOE.** It's the oldest form there is. Not very patriotic of you.

**DRUMBLE.** There is the matter of the people. And the people want a ballad.

*(a beat)*

Don't mock me, Joe.

**JACOB.** How are people treating you?

**ELIZABETH.** Respectfully.

**JACOB.** I walked past the farm this morning. Someone threw an apple core.

**ELIZABETH.** That's to be expected.

**JACOB.** They think I raped her. A lot of people think that, I guess.

(**DANIEL** *sings a jaunty tune as he skins his rabbit.*)

**DANIEL.** *(singing)*
> I took my little girl for a stroll in the fall,
> All that I thought about was a piece of tail.
> In a nice shady bower she agreed to take a rest
> And I gently slipped my hand upon her cuckoo's nest.

**JOE.** Susanna Cox.....What rhymes with Cox....?

**DRUMBLE.** Fox!

**JACOB.** I held him, after they found him. After they found him I went in there and I held him.

**ELIZABETH.** Good for you.

**JOE.** *(reading)* How do you pronounce his name? Jacob Gehr? Or Geer? It will affect the rhyme.

**DRUMBLE.** I don't know, find out.

**JOE.** Geer... leer....Gehr... dare...

**DRUMBLE.** An iniquitous pair!

**JOE.** Hair.... lair...

**DRUMBLE.** Oh that's good. Lair! And her the fox!

**CHAPLAIN.** *(to SUSANNA)* Here, in this dark place, you and I are going to pray together. We're going to pray as hard as we can. We will sleep very little, we will eat very little. We'll spend most of the time on our knees. And it will be hard.

But in two weeks you will be forced to leave this world and journey into the next. There you will meet God. You're not to be frightened. It's a journey we'll all take some day. You did a terrible thing. But I believe that God... and the governor of Pennsylvania... have given us enough time for you to be reborn.

*(a beat)*

Time has nothing to do with the days of the week or the months of the year. It slows up, it speeds down, I'm sure you've noticed this yourself.

Time has nothing to do with clocks.

**JOE.** I forgot to ask. How much do you want on the trial?

**DRUMBLE.** Three stanzas. Then her repentance in prison, repentance on the scaffold, moral summary. The end.

**SUSANNA.** *(on her knees, to herself)* I murdered my babe by the light of the moon
And they'll hang me on high when the church bell strikes noon.

**ELIZABETH.** What are you doing?

**JACOB.** I'm just finishing some letters.

**ELIZABETH.** To who?

**JACOB.** Lewis. Jefferson. Try and explain myself before word spreads.

**ELIZABETH.** Does our president really need to know what you've been up to?

**JACOB.** I'm sure he reads the papers. He is the president.

**ELIZABETH.** How do you explain yourself? In the letters?

**SUSANNA.** *(still on her knees, chanting)* He bent me this way that way forwards backwards, till only the stars I did see...Then I sucked on his prick, my flue he did lick and we both cried fiddle-de-de...

**JACOB.** I say I was foolish. That I had been very depressed. I say how sorry I am, for all the harm caused. Couldn't have predicted it.

*(a beat)*

**ELIZABETH.** Lewis is dead. Don't you read the papers?

**JACOB.** How?

**ELIZABETH.** He killed himself.

*(a beat)*

It's late. Come to bed.

**DANIEL.** *(singing jauntily,)*
Some like a girl who is pretty in the face
And some like a girl who is slender in the waist
Oh but give me a girl, who'll wriggle and will twist
At the bottom of the belly lies the cuckoo's nest.

*(**JACOB** watches as **ELIZABETH** prays by her bed.)*

**ELIZABETH.** Our Father, which art in heaven, Hallowed be Thy Name. Thy kingdom come. Thy will be done, in earth as it is in heaven. Give us this day our daily bread. And forgive us our trespasses, as we forgive them that trespass against us…

*(to Jacob)*

Feel free to join in….

*(a beat)*

… and lead us not into temptation; But deliver us from evil; for thine is the kingdom, the power and the glory, forever and ever amen

*(a beat)*

I would have preferred it if you'd raped her. Isn't that terrible?

**DANIEL.** *(singing, jaunty)*

My darling, it's not committing sin

But common sense should tell you it is a pleasing thing

You're brought into this world to increase and do your best

To take a man to heaven in your cuckoo's nest.

**SUSANNA.** *(still on her knees)* What are you going to do to me?

## SECOND MOVEMENT: THE HAUNTED

(**DANIEL** *starts cooking his rabbit.*)

**JOE.** I walk a pastoral paradise,
American fields heavy with...
He breaks off.

(*a beat*)

One thing at a time.

(*a beat*)

Jail....tale... wail.

(*a beat*)

Cell, hell, knell, bell.

**CHAPLAIN / SUSANNA.** Heavenly Father...
You understand all errors,
You forgive all sins...

**JOE.** Death... Breath....

(**SUSANNA** *can't remember the words to the prayer.*)

**CHAPLAIN.** And generously restore Your grace to those who
turn to You in repentance.

(*a beat*)

I know you can't read. That's a challenge for us. Because
for prayer, Susanna, we often use other people's words.
Other people, poets really, have already found a voice
for you. They have written your despair. They have written your regret. They have written your heartbreak. I'd
like to teach you some of those prayers.

I'd like you to know them by heart. I'd like you to
repeat them again and again. And in repetition will
come understanding.

(**SUSANNA** *and the* **CHAPLAIN** *repeat the same prayer
again together, quietly, a meditation, underneath* **JACOB**
*and* **ELIZABETH**.

**CHAPLAIN/SUSANNA.** Heavenly Father... Heavenly Father...
You understand all errors,
You forgive all sins....

**ELIZABETH.** *(repeating the chain of events to herself.)*

I woke up. I came down the stairs. She served us break-
fast. And then I heard the boys from the farm shouting.
I went to the window. There was blood on the snow...

*(a beat)*

Why didn't she come to me?

**JACOB.** You would have turned her out. She would have
starved to death.

**ELIZABETH.** I could have looked after it.

**JACOB.** A bastard child? Really? A child cursed by God?
Who you believe in? A child brought into this world by
fornication? The product of lust and foul debasement?
Of our two cracked and blackened souls rubbing
together? That child? You would have looked after it?

**JOE.** *(reading to Drumble)*

As married man he her seduced,

And brought her in distress

He may repent if not refused

At some time after death.

She had this matter not revealed

So much ashamed was she

She thought no person would take note

Of her delivery.

**DRUMBLE.** Can't you do better than that? Tighten up the
metre at least. Alright then what?

**JOE.** Then blinded sorely by her sin

And in her sorrow wild

This wicked mother raised her hand

And slew her new born child.

**DRUMBLE.** Fine... Next?

*(a beat)*

**JOE.** That's as far as I've got.

*(a beat)*

What does it matter? Everyone's saying she'll get off...

**DRUMBLE.** We have to be prepared.

**JOE.** I'm trying to work on the Epic too, you know.

**DRUMBLE.** Not until you've finished this. We have to be prepared.

**SUSANNA.** Wash me thoroughly from my wickedness, and cleanse me from my sin....

For I acknowledge my faults and....

**CHAPLAIN.** My sin is ever before me.

**SUSANNA.** My sin is ever before me... Against thee only have I sinned, and done this evil in Thy sight...

**CHAPLAIN.** Behold, I was shapen in wickedness, and in sin hath my mother conceived me...

**SUSANNA.** Behold, I was shapen in wickedness, and in sin hath my mother conceived me....

*(a beat)*

But lo, thou requirest truth in the inward parts, and shalt make me to understand wisdom secretly

*(a beat)*

Thou shalt purge me with...

**JACOB.** We made love against that wall...

**CHAPLAIN.** Hyssop...

**SUSANNA.** Hyssop... and I shall be...

**CHAPLAIN.** Clean; thou shalt wash me, and I shall be....

**JACOB.** Whiter than snow.

**CHAPLAIN.** Exactly.

*(a beat)*

Excuse me.

**DRUMBLE.** *(to the Chaplain, surprised)* We've met before.

**CHAPLAIN.** Yes, sir. You published my –

**DRUMBLE.** The Eden Sermon. It was excellent! Wonderfully ominous.

**CHAPLAIN.** Thanks very much.

**DRUMBLE.** I'm here to collect your sermon on the scaffold.

**CHAPLAIN.** My what?

**DRUMBLE.** For the hanging of Miss Cox. You have yet to deliver it to me.

**CHAPLAIN.** I haven't written it.

**DRUMBLE.** What's the matter with everybody?

**CHAPLAIN.** I'm hoping you won't need it.

**DRUMBLE.** Won't need it? It is a vital part of the package! His ballad, your sermon, her signed confession and her dying words. A significant amount of reading material needs to be amassed for the public!

**CHAPLAIN.** I have delivered a favorable report on the state of her soul to the governor... There is an appeal...

**DANIEL.** *(singing)*
Rabbits roasted rabbits fried,
Rabbits boiled and rabbits dried,
Rabbits tender, Rabbits tough
Thank you Lord we've rabbits enough

**ELIZABETH.** *(a beat)* There are things I want to ask you. About what you did. And where you did it. And if you knew that she was pregnant.

**JACOB.** It was never in our bed.

*(a beat)*

I made a point of it.

**ELIZABETH.** Did you know that she was pregnant?

*(a beat)*

**JACOB.** Yes.

**SUSANNA.** Imagine me naked. Just for a second.

**JACOB.** After what you did? I mustn't.

**JOE.** How did this even happen?

**SUSANNA.** Imagine me naked.

**JACOB.** I am.

**ELIZABETH.** *(an explosion)* I'm sorry I couldn't have any children! I'm sorry you hate it here so much! I don't know why you don't just leave me! Except I do know why. It's because you're a coward! And you haven't any money! And you don't know what you'd do with your-self because nobody wants you! Nobody ever wanted you but me! And that wasn't good enough!

**JACOB.** That's not true!

**ELIZABETH.** I failed the casket test. I picked the wrong suitor. And so did she.

*(a beat)*

My God, so did she.

*(**DANIEL** sings the same song – but the tune has changed. Slow. Aching.)*

**DANIEL.** Through pasture and deserts and mountains I've roamed...

*(**SUSANNA** joins in. Slow. Aching. Almost a spiritual.)*

**SUSANNA / DANIEL.** *(singing)*
Ain't no state in this union I've found to call home...
So I'll keep on wandering till my journey's rest...
My only salvation is the cuckoo's nest...

**SUSANNA.** *(to Daniel)* I did everything wrong.

**DANIEL.** No you didn't.

**SUSANNA.** That's not true.

**DANIEL.** Is.

**SUSANNA.** Isn't.

**DRUMBLE.** *(out of breath)* I just came from the governor's house. He's in a terrible state..They arrested another girl last night.

**CHAPLAIN.** Why?

**DRUMBLE.** She did the same thing. Over in Lancaster.

**CHAPLAIN.** Killed a newborn?

**DRUMBLE.** It appears to be an epidemic. Epidemics require quarantine. Your sermon is a vital part of the inocula-tion. As is the ballad. Make it a priority, please. Only a few days left.

**JOE.** I can't write this. I don't even understand how this could happen. I don't even understand how this could happen! I don't even understand what I'm writing about.

*(a beat)*

Did he rape you? Did you love him? How long did it go on for? Did he help you plan the murder? Are you a lunatic? Are you sorry? Did you close your eyes? Was the baby crying? Did you cry? Were there animals out? Did owls keep watch? Did ants scatter when you dug in the earth to make a grave? What were you thinking out in the moonlight?

*(a beat)*

Why didn't you bury it better? Why kill the poor little bastard if you weren't even going to try and get away with it?

*(a beat)*

Can you sleep? What do you dream of? What if I'd been that boy?

**DANIEL.** I see moonlight. I see your shadow, mighty big. Monstrous large you were with your hand about its neck, crushing it against the earth. Blood soaked. Wild like a creature from the pit. Looked beautiful, Susanna. Most beautiful thing I ever saw.

*(a beat)*

Can't repent. Can't take it back.

**SUSANNA.** I know.

*(To the* **CHAPLAIN***)*

I heard... there's an appeal?

**CHAPLAIN.** It was denied.

**EVERYBODY.** *(except Susanna and Daniel)*
As soon as the discoverers saw
That murder had been dealt
She was arrested by the law
And asked to own her guilt.

Her agony ah who can tell

She knew the end was nigh
And that upon the scaffold she
A shameful death must die.

## THIRD MOVEMENT: THE CONDEMNED

*(Middle of the night.)*

**CHAPLAIN.** Try not to sleep. God doesn't want you to sleep now. Stay on your knees. As long as you can.

**JOE.** "Yellow, yellow, yellow, grey...
Turn around and look my way...
By the window, are you there...
Or are you only dust and air?

I do not even know your name...
Or if you're wild or if you're tame...
Or if I see you standing there...
From where I sit in yellow chair...

Asleep I feel you pass the wall...
Float through where sun and shadows fall...
And I see your hair is fair...
Just before you leave me there... "

I can't give him that. That's not a ballad.

**ELIZABETH.** *(muttering to herself)* The babe's bones picked at by barn sparrows! And you the mother-monster with never a care, did you think you could get away with murder? Dirty little harlot. What if you'd got away with it? Would it still be going on? In my father's house?

**JACOB.** Elizabeth?

**ELIZABETH.** *(muttering to herself)*
"A woman is a useful thing
She does the wash she does the wring
But do not trust her with your heart
For lying is a woman's art."

**JACOB.** Are you awake?

**ELIZABETH.** That rhyme. It keeps going around in my head. My grandpa used to say it and my grandma would laugh.

**SUSANNA.** Daniel?

**CHAPLAIN.** *(half asleep, sermon unfinished)* Did you say Daniel?

**JACOB.** Elizabeth?

**ELIZABETH.** Yes?

**JACOB.** You sounded like you were crying...

**JOE.** Can I see Miss Susanna Cox?

**CHAPLAIN.** I'm sorry. No more visitors now.

**JOE.** But I'm her balladeer.

**CHAPLAIN.** She has very little time left. She's not spending it with a minstrel, I'm sorry.

**JOE.** I'm not a minstrel! I'm a poet. And I need to finish this ballad, because I have a lot of other things to do, and I can't finish unless I talk to her because –

**CHAPLAIN.** *(angry)* A poet? Cheap. You are cheap, sir. Make a pretty penny, profit off a tragedy, you are a rhymer sir and nothing more.

**JOE.** Sir, I assure you –

**CHAPLAIN.** Don't call yourself a poet, there is nothing cheap about a poet, the poet hears the music of the spheres and writes it down and is seldom paid enough to keep him in new neckties, sir!

*(He flicks at Joe's tie)*

You are a profiteer and she will not waste a second on you!

**JOE.** But I am how she will be remembered...

**CHAPLAIN.** Her concern is not with her reputation on earth.

**SUSANNA.** Do you believe in hell?

**DANIEL.** Can't be so bad. You'd get used to it. It goes on forever. People like us, we can get used to anything. I spent months in the wilderness. Just me and the wolves. All by myself. Hard. Lonely. I survived it. That's all you've got to do. Survive.

**JACOB.** If you pray for her soul and she goes to heaven, and then you go to heaven, does that mean the two of you would meet there? And then what? Will you embrace as angels?

(**ELIZABETH** *slaps him.*)

**ELIZABETH.** Maybe you're right! Maybe God doesn't exist at all! Maybe we should all be like the Indians and run around and play all day and worship whatever we want! Worship the sun, the moon, the stars! Maybe we should still be worshipping Zeus! I don't know!

*(The* **CHAPLAIN** *hands* **DRUMBLE** *his sermon.)*

**DRUMBLE.** I hear she's the picture of virtue. Doesn't eat, hardly sleeps, prays all day.

**CHAPLAIN.** It's true.

**DRUMBLE.** Believe her?

**CHAPLAIN.** She dreams of Daniel.

**DRUMBLE.** Daniel?

**CHAPLAIN.** The prophet.
  "And when she was led to be put to death, the Lord raised up the holy spirit of a young boy, whose name was Daniel… "
  It's from the Book of Susanna, in which Daniel saves Susanna from execution.
  It's apocryphal . There's no earthly way our Susanna could know of it. And yet she dreams of Daniel.
  She's calling out for God.

**DANIEL.** Three days, Susanna.

**JOE.** They're building the scaffold.

*(a beat)*

The city's filling up. I'm out of time.

*(Pause.)*

**SUSANNA.** If there is a God he won't like me. I did everything wrong. Shouldn't have touched that man, shouldn't have touched him. Wasn't supposed to touch myself either. Shouldn't have done that. Felt good though. Got to be a habit. Seems like I'd feel God, just for a second, end of my finger.
  Meant something to me.
  If you didn't want me to do it why didn't you stop me?

**DANIEL.** I did want you to do it.

**SUSANNA.** Not you then. God. Why didn't he stop me?
I waited for him. I listened for him. Thought I heard him sometimes too. Go outside, he'd say. Watch the wind make the corn dance.
So I did. I'd just stand there.
What did you want from me, standing there?

**DRUMBLE.** Twenty thousand people. Twenty thousand copies. Tell me you have thirty two stanzas!

(**JOE** *hands him a manuscript.*)

**SUSANNA.** Does God want me to die?

**CHAPLAIN.** I don't know. It wasn't his decision.

**DANIEL.** You'll be high up. You'll be able to see right over the city and out to the hills.

**SUSANNA.** Maybe I could come back as a ghost... There's research about it.

**DANIEL.** You're gonna step up there. You're gonna shut your eyes as quick as you can. And when you do you'll see a little dot of light somewhere. You know what that is?

*(a beat)*

That's the horizon. That's where I'll be. Waiting for you.

**DRUMBLE.** Imagine it! An extraordinary number of people. People in every branch of every tree as far as the eye can see. Roofs full. People standing on carriages. Every person you could ever imagine will be there. Hunchbacks, merchants, the finest women you ever saw. Doctors, lawyers, young men sitting on each other's shoulders! The sun beating down! Babies crying! Horses kicking at the crowd!
The chaplain will say his sermon, which we are printing, no one will listen! Everyone will be jostling, struggling for position, all straining for the sight of you!
Susanna, you will step forward. You will silence Philadelphia. What will you say to them, standing there?

**CHAPLAIN.** Anything she says at that point will be a prayer. She won't be able to help it. What else could she possibly say?

**SUSANNA.** I'm sorry.

**JACOB.** I'm sorry too.
We should have run away. Far west. I could have taken some money. Got us on a stage to Kentucky! Outlaws. I'd have built you a house.

**SUSANNA.** A log house.

**JACOB.** Yes.

*(a beat)*

*(**DANIEL** dresses **SUSANNA** in white.)*

**EVERYBODY.** *(except Susanna and Daniel)*
She knelt upon the earth in prayer
And asked the Lord Alone
That he would all her sins forgive
Which ever she had done.

Her weeping was so sorrowful
As on her knees she lay
Her tear drops fell upon the earth
They wept for her that day.

**SUSANNA.** Do you ever think you'll get into trouble? For what you did to the Indians?

**DANIEL.** Just did what I had to do.

**DRUMBLE.** *(reading)*
"From prison she was taken out
About eleven o'clock
Unto the execution place
It caused a mortal shock.

She cautioned all mankind around
The young especially.
And said "take an example now
By my ill fate today."

Joe, this doesn't sound anything like you at all...

*(a beat)*

I'd expected more.

*(a beat)*

Something about this feels terribly familiar…

*(A beat)*

JOE. Some of it's the ballad of Henny Finch. I just changed the names. Nobody will remember. You didn't.

*(a beat)*

I'm sorry but I just couldn't… I couldn't finish it…

DRUMBLE. It was hard for you. Accepting a young thing like that could commit such an act in this great country of ours.

JOE. Yes, sir. I write a different America.

DRUMBLE. You do.

JOE. Even so, the ballad has sold every copy. They are singing it in the streets. I've done my job. And also….
I have the second installment of my Epic.

SUSANNA. My throat hurts.

ELIZABETH. She must have been very tired. Otherwise she would have buried the baby better.

*(a beat)*

I worry I jeopardize my soul in loving you.

*(a beat)*

It's noon.

JACOB. It's noon.

DANIEL. It's noon, Susanna. It's time.

ELIZABETH. She'll get to find out if God exists…

ELIZABETH/CHAPLAIN. Our father who art in heaven…

*(They continue praying)*

DANIEL. You're gonna walk, you're gonna climb. They'll put a bag on your head. And you'll fall. And everything's going to be alright.

**JACOB.** *(joining in)* For thine is the kingdom the power and the glory forever and ever, Amen.

**CHAPLAIN.** *(to his congregation)* Who was Mary Magdalen? A prostitute. What does that mean? None of us are just one person. Our bones grow and shrink as seasons pass. We live through forms we can barely remember. We look back and see ourselves as indistinct. Distant. Different now.

May god have mercy on *all* our souls.

**JOE.** What do you think of the second installment?

**DRUMBLE.** You must work it again, Joe. There's something not quite right about it. I don't know...

**JACOB.** *(desperate)* It must be over by now...

**ELIZABETH.** Yes. Yes it must be. It must be.

**DRUMBLE.** The tone is... something's changed...

*(a beat)*

Look at her kick.

*(a beat)*

I remember when I saw my first hanging, I was only eight years old. It was before the war. I was English then, I suppose. And my father lifted me onto his shoulders and he said...

*(Something shifts. Perhaps lights, perhaps staging...but something. Susanna has disappeared. We see the rest of the cast for what they are: actors dressed in the faded costumes of the past.)*

**DRUMBLE.** Getting old....I don't remember...

## End of Play